I GIFT THIS CUTE AND MELLOW BOOK

TO

_____

FROM

_____

Cabbie the Cannabis Leaf Goes to Washington, D.C.

By Randy Sarul

Children's Stories for Childish Adults

Author Randy Sarul
Editor Namrok

I dedicate this book

to the loving memory of my two sisters whose way of life was rooted in Philotimo.

It was a rare honor for the random choice of the universe to have blessed me with the opportunity to be their little sister. I thank them for the experiences and love we shared.

My treasure chest of memories is rich with the twinkling jewels of these two and many other loving family members that have gone before me.

May their memories be eternal.

Love with gratitude and thankfulness

Lil Na

TABLE OF CONTENTS

Cabbie the Cannabis Leaf Goes to Washington, D.C.

By Randy Sarul

Intro

Cabbie the Cannabis Leaf lives and grows in a community garden, in a neighborhood near you. He grows alongside other natural and organic fruits, vegetables, and herbs.

The Cannabis Clan has played a great part in the making of not only the Americas but in World history; the Cannabis Clan's contributions have been vast.

You are about to learn some of these rarely spoken of facts and contributions in history while you travel along with Mother Mary Jane and Cabbie, as Cabbie Goes to Washington, D.C.

Spring Happenings

Springtime had fallen upon the land and the community garden was all a buzz. Bees were busy flying about pollinating everything in sight, making sure the garden would be in full bloom throughout the season.

Sproutlings were waking up, popping their little heads out from under the soil for "with spring comes new life." Budlings were playing and swaying delighting in the golden rays of the spring sunshine while drinking in the early morning dew.

As the garden was active with spring activities, Cabbie and his Mother Mary Jane were busy too. Mary Jane had surprised Cabbie and told him they were going to spend spring break in Washington, D.C. at the National Mall.

Though Cabbie and his clan have become somewhat of a hero in our world today it wasn't always this way. Cabbie spent many years being profiled and bullied. Some of these bullies taunted him, calling him names, yelling out "Cabbie is a noid! Cabbie is a noid!"

Mother Mary Jane felt it was time Cabbie learned about his ancestors, the Cannabis Clan, and their great contributions in the founding of our country.

Mary Jane wanted to make Cabbie feel better and to help him understand he was created for a purpose as are each and every one of us. She thought by showing Cabbie some of the great contributions made in history by his ancestors, he might look toward his future with more confidence and excitement.

Mother Mary Jane told Cabbie their family played an intricate part in the success and building of the new world, America. What a great heritage, Cabbie thought to himself when he heard this. "Mother, please tell me more," Cabbie eagerly asked.

"Clearly, the Cannabis history is rich in America as our ancestor's contributions were unwavering, so I thought it a good idea to learn firsthand. That is why we are going to Washington, D.C.," Mother Mary Jane told him. Cabbie was curious to think of all the many historical things he would learn within the walls of the museums in the Smithsonian Institute on the National Mall in Washington, D.C.

Mother Mary Jane was also excited to think of how Cabbie would be discovering the many significant additions and improvements his ancestors, the Cannabis Clan, made not just in American history but since the beginning of time.

Mother Mary Jane wanted her son to be proud of his ancestors and to learn not only of their sufferings and struggles but their contributions and donations as well. It would be the perfect history lesson disguised as a vacation, Mary Jane thought to herself as she and Cabbie continued, with great anticipation, to prepare for their fun and learned vacation in Washington, D.C.

Cherry Blossoms on the National Mall

Mother Mary Jane and Cabbie's first morning on the National Mall was a glorious morning. The sky painted the background for the beautiful Cherry blossoms that were in full bloom. It was magnificent and picture perfect, such a wondrous site. The Cherry Blossom trees only bloom in spring. Mother Mary Jane had timed their trip just right.

Mary Jane and Cabbie felt blessed and honored to stand together taking in such a lovely site. What a great way to start their vacation on the National Mall in Washington, D.C.

Cabbie watched his mother as she gazed at the beauty of the blossoms. She seemed deeply emotional. Cabbie asked his mother why the Cherry blossoms were so important to her, was it their beauty? Mother Mary Jane exclaimed not only because they were beautiful but that they were a gift from the Chinese people.

Mother Mary Jane said this was significant to her as the first historical records of Cabbie's ancestors can be found in the artifacts of the oldest known culture in China, the Neolithic Yangshao people who date back to 5000 BC. Mary Jane thought it proud that the ancestors of the Cannabis Clan were known to have assisted and provided the Yangshao people with many of their basic needs such as shampoo, clothing, rope, and medicine, as well as assisting with their shamanic practices, among other things.

Mother Mary Jane told Cabbie, "When I stand before these beautiful Cherry blossoms, I feel a deep connection as our ancestors were a part of this ancient Chinese culture and their history".

The Cherry Blossoms, as magnificent as they are, were just the beginning of their journey. There was much more to see and learn so Cabbie and his mother decided to make a plan as there are many museums to visit on the National Mall.

There is the National Museum of American History, the National Gallery of Art, the Library of Congress, the United States Botanical Gardens and the National Postal Museum, just to name a few.

Cabbie and Mother Mary Jane decided they would start with the National Museum of American History. Cabbie and Mom then grabbed a cool organic and nutritional drink before starting off on their journey. Both were filled with great anticipation of the treasures they would find while walking through these sacred halls of history.

Treasure Hunt

Cabbie had been told of the rich treasures he would find in history about his clan. He wasn't sure why Mother Mary Jane thought they would find any such thing in the National Museum of American History, but he didn't care. He wanted to see anything concerning America's first President, George Washington. President Washington has long been one of Cabbie's favorite historical heroes.

Suddenly, there it was, the George Washington statue in all its glory. Washington's likeness was detailed and surreal. Cabbie stood speechless before the statue. Just about that time he heard his mother exclaim, "Washington was a great friend of our Clan as were many other American Presidents". Cabbie looked at her curiously.

Cabbie soon learned President Washington's farm in Mount Vernon was home to many of Cabbie's ancestors. Yes, George Washington not only grew Hemp, which is a particular type of cannabis, but promoted it too.

Cabbie saw a letter while at the museum that was written by President Washington to his plantation manager, William Pearle. President Washington wrote, "Make the most of the Indian hemp seed and sow it everywhere". Indian Hemp was the common name for cannabis at this particular time in history.

Cabbie also learned President Thomas Jefferson is quoted saying, "Hemp is of first necessity to the wealth and protection of the country". Cabbie shouted, "Mother! You mean our ancestors?"

"Unquestionably son, the Cannabis Clan has done many good and honorable things for America," Mother Mary Jane stated.

Cabbie learned the 2nd American President, John Adams, and the 5th American President, James Monroe, promoted the Cannabis Clan and the use of it. Cabbie and his mother saw an oil lamp President Abraham Lincoln used for reading. The lamp was said to have been fueled by hemp oil. Yes, Cabbie's ancestors even fueled President Abraham Lincoln's reading lamp. Guess you could say, "The Cannabis Clan lit the way!"

Cabbie then stood before preserved letters he found on exhibit while in the National Museum of American History. Each of the three letters was penned by a different military man who had written home to tell their families how one time unexpectedly in the evening after fighting a long day on the battle field, President Andrew Jackson came and sat with the men around the camp fire to give them support and shared with them the calming effects of Cannabis at the end of what was a harsh and difficult day.

Cabbie thought to himself, "even in the worst of times my ancestors were providing comfort and relief to those in need". Cabbie was beginning to feel very proud of his heritage and his ancestral history.

Cabbie and Mother Mary Jane found many precious treasures while at the National Museum of American History. What might they find next?

Cannabis in the New World

Cabbie and Mother Mary Jane saw many things inside the National Museum of American History, but the things Cabbie took away and remembered the most were the facts about how the Cannabis Clan was America's legal tender during the start of the new world.

When the British finally left New York in 1777, America had not yet established a legal currency. In other words, America had no money. Hemp served as a form of legal tender for the first several years. Prior to this time when the settlers were still under the control of the British by decree of King James I in 1619, the colonists were made to grow 100 hemp plants per year for export as their lot.

Colonists were legally bound to grow hemp for the King during the colonial period or be arrested, jailed or even deported from the Americas. Colonists were also required in the early republic of the new world, when no longer under British rule, to grow hemp as it was mandate by law.

Indian Hemp growth was vital for the survival of the colonists. Hemp production served in producing sails for ships, rope, and paper. Oil for lamps, clothing, and shampoo were among the other necessities the Cannabis Clan contributed. Many years later in America, during World War II, American citizens were encouraged to grow hemp for the war effort.

Before moving on to the next museum, while Old Ironsides resides at the USS Constitution Museum, Cabbie and Mother saw information about this naval vessel. They learned she is the oldest commissioned naval vessel still afloat today. Her lines, rigging, and sails are all made of cannabis hemp fiber. One of the great contributions to the Navy from the Cannabis Clan has been in the construction of the USS Constitution, Old Ironsides.

Cabbie and Mother Mary Jane found that almost 55 tons of cannabis hemp fiber resin was used to caulk the wooden hull of this naval vessel. Old Ironsides was given her name because cannonballs bounced off the hull of the USS Constitution. It is believed this is because of the quality of the cannabis caulk.

Cabbie, feeling emotional and overwhelmed, looked at his mother with amazement and said, "Gee mom, I never realized what a strong history we have."

Cabbie began wondering, "If this much of our family history can be found in the National Museum of American History, just imagine what other treasures concerning our Cannabis Clan might be found in some of the other museums."

Excited to learn more, Cabbie asked, "Where to next mom?" After carefully looking at the map, they decided the National Gallery of Art would be their next adventure.

Cannabis History and the National Gallery of Art

There is nothing quite like the visual beauty and mental stimulation of taking in a great art exhibit. Imagine standing in front of a sculpture created in the thirteenth century or a rare painting from the nineteenth century, how chilling it might be.

The National Gallery of Art holds a variety of things to see from modern day marvels to the great Renaissance Masters. Cabbie had no idea that these wonderful gems awaited him inside the doors of this museum.

Cabbie and Mother Mary Jane tried to see everything the National Gallery of Art had to offer, from the sculpture gardens to artwork that has survived for hundreds of years. They saw thought provoking works filled with creativity and colors as each piece tells a different story to those who gaze upon them. It was a visual buffet for the eyes to feast upon.

Cabbie and Mother Mary Jane soon found themselves standing before the Nineteenth-

Century French Gallery. This particular exhibit features work by some of the most renowned painters in history such as Monet, Renoir, and Vincent van Gogh. It was here Cabbie learned that the Nineteenth-Century French Gallery was literally dripping with history of the Cannabis Clan.

While feeling humble and thankful to view these masterpieces, Cabbie listened and learned how most, if not all, of Vincent van Gogh's paintings were created on canvas made from the hemp of the Cannabis Clan. It is amazing to know Cabbie's ancestors provided the canvas on which these masterpieces were created.

Painting on hemp canvas supported oil better than did using oil paint on a linen canvas. Hemp canvas remains flexible longer and does not stretch and shrink like linen.

Monet, Renoir, and several of the great artists of yesterday created their work on hemp canvas. It was the most used material for canvas until the mid-1800's when hemp production in France declined.

Even the name canvas came from the root word Cannabis. Yes, canvases were given this name because they were made of cannabis.

It was one thing to stand before the work of such historical, integral painters, but it was another thing to learn the Cannabis Clan contributed to the making of these masterpieces. Cabbie felt chills and goose pimples rise up his stem.

The United States Botanical Gardens

Presidents George Washington, Thomas Jefferson, and James Madison shared a dream, a vision to create a total collection of every plant from around the world. This shared idea was the seed child of The United Stated Botanical Gardens. This is where a great collection of nature's magnificent works of art can be found all in one place.

Oddly enough, the Cannabis Clan is not represented among the collection of rare and unique plants at this time, but the dream for the United States Botanical Gardens these Presidents had is alive and growing ever more complete.

There are a few living plants that can be dangerous if used wrong and are illegal in most countries. These illicit plants are not on exhibit in any of the United States Botanical Gardens for good reason.

There are other categories of plants that are not on display due to fear and misunderstanding of the plant such as the Cannabis Clan. With all the contributions the Cannabis Clan has made throughout history, it is heart breaking to think Cannabis has been given such a bad rap.

After all, cannabis was one of the main crops grown by President George Washington at his home in Mt. Vernon. Benjamin Franklin and Presidents Thomas Jefferson and James Madison, not only farmed cannabis, but promoted it as well.

The contributions by the Cannabis Clan have clearly been productive and helpful making the Cannabis Clan one of the plants that has certainly earned its place in the great botanical exhibit. Perhaps in time, the Cannabis Clan will help the United States Botanical Gardens grow by becoming part of its community and vast displays.

The Pentagon

While the United States Botanical Gardens won't allow an exhibit of the Cannabis Clan, Cabbie's Mother, Mary Jane, told him the legacy of their ancestors lies deep in the rich Virginia soil under one of the national symbols of our United States Government, The Pentagon.

Cabbie learned that Cannabis was once grown and researched by the United States Government in Washington, D.C. at Arlington Farm, where the Pentagon stands today.

A botanist name Lyster Dewey did extensive research and breeding with hemp and other fiber crops from 1903 until Arlington Farm closed in 1940, making way for the building of the Pentagon. It has been said that Lyster Dewey was the tender of Uncle Sam's Hemp Farm.

Ironically, where hemp was once grown by the United States government now sits the parking lot for the Pentagon, located right across the street from the Drug Enforcement Administration Headquarters. The headquarters of the same men in suits with dogs that hunted and caged friends of the Cannabis Clan and pillaged and burned their village the night Grandfather Cannab was snuffed out.

Cabbie enjoyed learning about Arlington Farm and the Pentagon. While Cabbie and Mother were not able to visit the Pentagon, as it is in Arlington, Virginia, Cabbie tried to imagine what it might have looked like to see his ancestors stretching across the land naturally swaying and waving in unison from the winds of the evening as the sunset glowed behind them. What a site it must have been.

The National Postal Museum

Inside the National Postal Museum, Cabbie and his mother viewed a rare stamp on exhibit, the Marihuana Tax Act of 1937 Stamp. The United States Congress passed the Marihuana Tax Act of 1937 to place taxes on the sale and growth of cannabis.

While this stamp did not prohibit marijuana, it did place restrictions on growers that were harsh and unreasonable. Growers were required to grow their hemp crops without leaves or flowers. Obviously, this made growing cannabis impossible as it would with any crop.

The Marihuana Tax Act of 1937 taxation was huge, and this too made it impractical to grow cannabis. It drove the cost to consumers too high, thus shutting down the growth, production, and distribution of cannabis in America.

The Pentagon, the National Postal Museum, even the Botanical Gardens possess great knowledge and preserved facts about our Cannabis Clan throughout history, Cabbie thought to himself.

Cabbie was beginning to feel a little overwhelmed by the history of his ancestors, but he was eager to find what new and interesting facts were around the next corner. "Gee Mom," Cabbie exclaimed, "Is there a museum on the National Mall our clan isn't in?"

"I don't know son", Mother answered with a chuckle, "let's continue on and find out."

The Library of Congress

What a beautiful day on the National Mall for Cabbie and Mother Mary Jane, but the day wasn't over yet. Mother Mary Jane told Cabbie the next stop, and their last stop, was the Library of Congress.

Mother explained the Library of Congress is the largest library in the world, with millions of books, recordings, photographs, newspapers, maps, and manuscripts in its collections. Cabbie loves books, so this was an unexpected surprise; it filled him with great anticipation.

Mother knew how exciting it would be for Cabbie to be among such a collection of books inside the Library of Congress. She leaned over to Cabbie and sweetly kissed him on the cheek and said, "Son, that is why I saved the best for last; I knew it would make you happy".

Upon entering the Library of Congress, one of the first things Cabbie noticed was a special exhibit that was temporarily on display of Mark Twain's work. Cabbie not only loves books and reading, but

Mark Twain happened to be one of Cabbie's favorite authors. Cabbie has two Mark Twain books at home and wanted to learn more about him, so off to the Mark Twain exhibit Mother Mary Jane and Cabbie went.

Cabbie and Mom soon learned that Mark Twain was born Samuel Langhorne Clemens. Mark Twain is the pen name used by Mr. Clemens. Mark Twain is a nautical reference that means two fathoms deep. Learning this left Cabbie wondering why Mr. Clemens picked this particular name.

Cabbie learned that Mark Twain's first great novel, *The Adventures of Huckleberry Finn*, was produced on cannabis hemp fiber, as were all of Mark Twain's publications. "Gee Whiz Mom!" Cabbie exclaimed. "Our ancestors helped make these works of literary art possible. Our Cannabis Clan is part of Mark Twain's legacy! Wait until I tell our family and friends back home".

Cabbie learned other great literary treasures were produced on cannabis hemp fiber, such as Victor Hugo's, *The Hunchback of Notre-Dame*, Alexander Dumas', *The Man in the Iron Mask* and *The Count of Monte Cristo*, plus Lewis Carroll's masterpiece, *Alice in Wonderland*.

Children and adults alike have read and passed down from generation to generation these brilliant and creative books that would not have been possible without contributions of the Cannabis Clan. Cabbie wondered if his generation would bring forth such historical contributions as his ancestors had in the past.

Cabbie went on to learn about another book which his ancestors took part in the production of, and that book was the *Bible*. This came as a big surprise to Cabbie.

Cabbie learned that the *King James Bible* and the *Gutenberg Bible* were the two most highly produced books in history. They were also originally printed on paper made from cannabis hemp fiber. Cabbie found this fascinating.

Mother Mary Jane began explaining to Cabbie that in today's world access to the *Bible* is easy and the book of the *Bible* can be found anywhere and in every language. She continued to tell Cabbie that this wasn't always the case.

Mother Mary Jane told Cabbie about a time when Christians were denied access to the *Bible*. It was considered heresy by the churches to read the *Bible* and was punishable by death. Yes, scriptures were sanctioned, and there was a prohibition forbidding translation of the *Bible* into native languages.

The *Bible*, for 1,000 years, was only written in Latin and only read by high ranking church officials. Many people suffered for centuries trying to free the *Bible* from its hidden place in the Church so all could read it for themselves. Their efforts were not in vain.

In 1450, Johann Gutenberg produced the first printing press and produced the first book. That book was the *Gutenberg Bible*. Yes, the first book printed was the *Bible* and it was created on Cannabis Hemp Fiber Paper.

In 1611, the *King James Bible*, also printed on hemp fiber paper, was distributed in several different languages. Mother Mary Jane asked Cabbie to take a minute and ponder how, with his ancestors help, the *Bible* was able to reach millions of people all over the globe and in each person's native language. Mother told Cabbie how this was a sacred and an anointed honor to have had the Cannabis Clan, Cabbie's ancestors, help make this possible.

Mother Mary Jane told Cabbie the next time someone profiles or bullies him to remember how he comes from a great line who participated in the mass production of the *Bible* for the first time in history.

Cabbie and Mother Mary Jane saw displays containing pamphlets that were sent out to the American people in 1933 urging citizens to grow hemp. They also noticed a featured publication in the 1938 issue of Popular Mechanics magazine about hemp titled, "Billion Dollar Crop", as they enjoyed their time inside the Library of Congress.

The Lyster Dewey Diaries were among the museum's collection. "Remember, Lyster Dewey studied hemp for the United States government in the early 1900's," Mother Mary Jane reminded Cabbie.

Cabbie asked, "You mean the tender of Uncle Sam's Hemp Farm?"

"Yes, that's the one," Mother replied.

Mother told Cabbie that many books about Cannabis lined the library shelves. One very popular book of the modern day was written by a visionary, John Heren, called, *The Emperor Wears No Clothes*. Cabbie just couldn't believe the extent of information that is logged within the halls of the Library of Congress concerning the history of the Cannabis Clan.

Mother Mary Jane suggested to Cabbie that perhaps one day there would be books on the shelves within the Library of Congress called *"Cabbie the Cannabis Leaf"* about all of Cabbie's adventures. Cabbie giggled and cleverly replied, "Yeah Mom, and the book will be published under Children's Stories for Childish Adults.

Mother smiled, laughed, and then replied, "One never knows Cabbie, for anything is possible." The two ended their time at the Library of Congress and the museums on the National Mall.

Looking to the Future as Spring Break Ends

The sun began to set behind the horizon illuminating, once again, the beauty of the Cherry Blossoms. Cabbie and Mother Mary Jane's time on the National Mall had come to an end.

At the close of this power packed day of information, Mother Mary Jane told Cabbie to be thankful for his great heritage. She told him to never forget the many services and contributions his ancestors, the Cannabis Clan, have provided in history and to treasure the many things he learned in the museums on the National Mall while in Washington, D.C.

Mother said, "Cabbie, be confident that in your lifetime you too will bring much to the world as those who have gone before you. Never doubt yourself or be hurt by those who finger point and bully you. Just remember, they do this out of fear of what they don't understand. Remain mellow and calm, show kindness to these people, for just as you learn and grow so will others by seeing the continual positive contributions our Cannabis Clan brings forth."

That night Cabbie's young mind had been set ablaze and his passion for looking forward set on fire. His thoughts filled with pride as he envisioned a time when famous Renaissance Artists lived and created great masterpieces. He felt giddy to know the canvases used to fashion priceless pieces of art were made from hemp and that canvases got their name from Cannabis.

Cabbie was swirling with joy and pride to think of how the Cannabis Clan helped in the success of the New World in its infancy by acting as America's first legal tender.

He daydreamed of the many Bibles that made their way to churches around the world.

He dreamt of the USS Constitution as it sailed into battle, as well as the unseen soldiers that forged the constitution of democracy all with Cabbie's ancestors by their side.

What an adventure Cabbie found on the National Mall in Washington, D.C. Most of all, Cabbie realized that while some will say the Cannabis Clan is bad, he will never doubt himself again after learning how important the Cannabis Clan has been in history and in knowing the great potential contributions the future holds for him and for all of the Cannabis Clan.

One of Cabbies proudest accomplishments has been helping Mr. Good Guy. The other is having taken the Organic Club Pledge.

You too can become part of the Organic Community by taking the Personal Pledge. The Organic Club pledge is, "**Always make natural, healthy, and organic choices when possible, and try to bring forth a healthier life not only for yourself but for the future of mankind.**"

If you find you like what you read, gift or share this cute and mellow Cabbie adventure with others. Be sure to take the Organic Club Pledge and Visit us at www.CabbieTheCannabisLeaf.com

You can learn more about Cabbie and his fantastic tales in Cabbies other adventures! Cabbies story does not end here.

www.ingramcontent.com/pod-product-compliance
Lightning Source LLC
Chambersburg PA
CBHW020609130626
46552CB00007B/3126